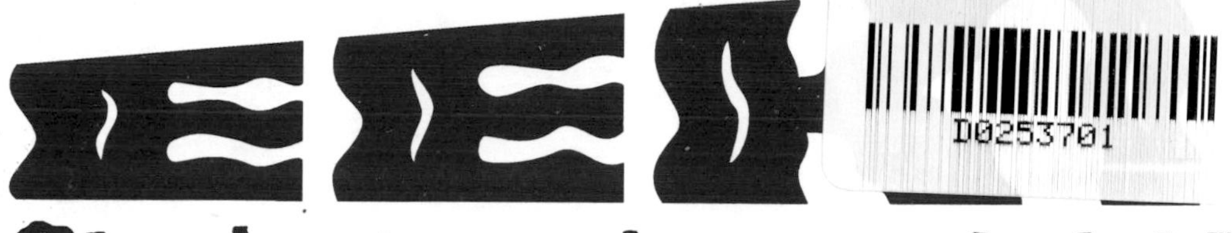

Stories to make you shriek™

For Beginning Readers
Ages 6-8

This series of spooky stories has been created especially for beginning readers—children in first and second grades who are developing their reading skills.

How do these books help children learn to read?

- Kids love creepy stories and these stories are true page-turners (but never too scary).
- The sentences are short.
- The words are simple and repeated often in the story.
- The type is large with lots of room between words and lines.
- Full-color pictures on every page act as visual "clues" to help children figure out the words on the page.

Once children have read one story, they'll be asking for more!

 Published by Grosset & Dunlap, Inc., which is a member of The Putnam & Grosset Group, New York. EEK! STORIES TO MAKE YOU SHRIEK is a trademark of The Putnam & Grosset Group. GROSSET & DUNLAP is a trademark of Grosset & Dunlap, Inc. Published simultaneously in Canada. Printed in the U.S.A.

Library of Congress Cataloging-in-Publication Data

Speregen, Devra.
The wax museum / by Devra Speregen ; illustrated by Donald Cook.
p. cm. — (Eek! Stories to make you shriek)
Summary: While lost in a creepy wax museum, Jordan has a strange encounter with one of its inmates.
[1. Museums—Fiction. 2. Horror stories.] I. Cook, Donald, ill. II. Title. III. Series.
PZ7.S7489Wax 1996
[Fic]—dc20 95-18328
CIP
AC

ISBN 0-448-41273-X A B C D E F G H I J

Easy-to-Read
Ages 6–8

The Wax Museum

By Devra Speregen
Illustrated by Donald Cook

Grosset & Dunlap • New York

Jordan Green looked out

her hotel window.

It was raining.

It rained a lot in London.

Her family was there on vacation.

"The rain will not stop us.
We will find something fun to do,"
said her father.
Jordan's brother Dan looked up
from his travel book.
"How about the wax museum?" he asked.

Wax museum?

Jordan felt a lump in her throat.

They had seen a poster

for the wax museum at the airport.

It looked really scary.

Dan had been talking about it ever since.

Jordan hated scary stuff.
And she never went to scary places
like museums filled with
creepy wax statues.
But Dan loved all that stuff.
And he had been so nice yesterday.
Dan had gone with Jordan
to a dollhouse museum.
Dan was such a nice brother.
So now Jordan did not want
to spoil his fun.

"Can we go, Mom?" Dan asked again.

Jordan's mother turned
and looked at Jordan.

It was as if she were saying,
"Is that okay with you?"

So Jordan said, "Sounds like fun."
And she tried to smile.

"Then it's off to

the wax museum we go!"

Dad said.

Jordan and her family
waited for a bus.
Jordan thought it was cool
the way the bus had an upstairs.

It was cool, too, the way

all the people talked.

Jordan listened to two men.

It was English.

But it sounded very different.

Lots of words were different, too.

Going to the loo meant

going to the bathroom.

Cookies were biscuits.

And policemen were called bobbies.

Jordan saw a bobby across the street.

"If you get lost here,"

her dad told her,

"just ask for help from a bobby."

Jordan nodded.

But she did not plan on getting lost

in a strange city.

That would be so scary!

AX MUSEUM

At the wax museum

the Greens waited in line for tickets.

Dan kept reading from his book.

“We get to see all kinds

of famous murderers!” he said.

"One guy cut up twenty-seven people into lots of little pieces! Look!"

Dan showed Jordan the picture.

"Cool!" Jordan said weakly.

"Jordan, remember,

you do not have to go inside,"

her dad said.

"I can take you someplace else

if you want."

But Jordan took her ticket.

"No. It's okay," she said.

"It's not like any of the stuff is real."

Inside the museum,

it was cold and damp

and very dark.

It looked like the streets

of London at night.

There were creepy wax statues everywhere.

Jordan did not like it at all.

But Dan was having a great time.

He stopped at every statue.

"Check it out! Jack the Ripper!" he cried.

"And look over here!

A headless man!"

Dan shouted.

Jordan could not help but look.

The headless man

was holding his head.

His dark eyes were still open.

They were staring right at her!

It's not real. . . .

It's not real. . . ,

Jordan told herself.

But the headless man

did not look like wax.

He looked real.

"Um, Mom, I think I have
to go to the bathroom,"
Jordan said.
That was not really true.
It was just an excuse to get away
for a little bit.
"I will be back in a minute."

There was an arrow.

It pointed to the bathrooms.

Her parents said they would wait

right where they were.

So Jordan followed the arrow,

and then another arrow.

Ah! There was the sign—

LADIES ROOM.

In she went.

Jordan took a few deep breaths.

She splashed some water on her face.

"You are acting like a baby,"

she told herself.

"Get a grip!"

It was just an old museum, after all.

A minute later Jordan came out.
She thought it would be easy
to retrace her steps.
But somehow
she was all turned around.
The museum was so dark.
The halls looked different now.

It suddenly hit Jordan

that she was all alone.

Just her and a room

full of wax monsters.

It felt as if she were being watched,

as if eyes were following her.

A shiver ran through Jordan.

Should she go left,

past the wax prisoner in handcuffs?

Where <u>was</u> her family?

As Jordan started to take a step,

something grabbed her arm.

Jordan closed her eyes and screamed.

AHHHH!

"Whoa there, little lady,"

a voice said.

Jordan opened her eyes.

Beside her was a policeman—

a bobby.

"Are you lost?" the bobby asked.

Jordan nodded.

She felt foolish now for screaming.

But the bobby was not laughing at her.

He seemed concerned.

The bobby had a very kind face.
He had rosy cheeks
and a big mustache
that drooped way down.

The bobby put his arm around Jordan.

"Not to worry," he said with a smile.

"This happens a lot.

The museum is like a maze.

Come with me.

I will help you find your family."

The way he said "maze"

sounded like "mize."

And he said "elp" instead of "help."

The bobby led Jordan

through the museum.

He kept talking in a friendly way.

He even let Jordan try on his hat.

Soon they were back in the room

with the headless man.

Jordan's eyes lit up.

There was her family!

"Mom! Dad! Dan!" she cried out,

and ran to them.

“Jordan!” her mother said.

“What took you so long?

We were starting to worry!”

“I got lost,” Jordan said.

Then she smiled.

"But this nice bobby helped me.

He let me try on his hat!"

Jordan's family looked puzzled.

"What bobby?" all three of them

asked at the same time.

Jordan turned around.

There was no one there.

The bobby was gone.

"He was here a second ago,"

Jordan told her family.

She felt bad.

She had wanted to thank the bobby.

Dad looked at his watch.

"Well, I think I have seen

enough monsters and murderers

for one day," he said.

"I'm ready for some tea and biscuits.

How about you guys?"

Jordan was only too glad

to leave the wax museum.

She followed her dad toward the exit.

Suddenly, Jordan noticed

someone up ahead.

It was a man in a blue uniform.

"I think it's him!" cried Jordan.

"The bobby who helped me!"

Jordan raced up to him.

He was standing beside

the wax prisoner in handcuffs.

“I wanted to thank—”

she started to say.

Then she stopped.

It was him.

The bobby had the same

droopy mustache.

But there was one big difference.

The bobby was made of wax!

How could it be?

The bobby had talked to her.

He had brought her back to her parents.

Jordan did not have an answer.

All she knew was

she had to get out of

the wax museum now.

Jordan turned to go.

She looked up at the bobby

one last time.

And he winked at her.